FALLING FOR THE PLUG 🏆

FALLING FOR THE PLUG

Table of Contents

Introduction

1. The Setup
2. The Yacht Date

3. The First Drop

4. Living the Double Life

5. New Bag, New Suspicions

6. Tension Rising

7. The Confrontation

8. Eyes Watching

9. Everything Unraveling

10. The Final Play

11. Narrated Outro: Lessons from the Game

Introduction

This story is based on real events.

Some names, locations, and details have been changed to protect the people involved — including the ones who still think they got away with it.

Every lie in this book is wrapped in a truth I've either lived, seen, or escaped from.

I didn't write this to glorify the game, but to show how it tricks you:

How it whispers like love but moves like betrayal.

Falling for the Plug isn't just about drugs, women, or fast money.

It's about how we get caught in things we never signed up for — and how easy it is to lose everything when we ignore the signs.

If you've ever thought about crossing that line — or already have — this book is for you.

Not to judge. But to warn.

— **Kevin T Gaskins**

Chapter 1: FBI Interrogation Room

Kevin's chest was tight, his breathing uneven. His pulse pounded in his ears, but no matter how much he tried to steady his nerves, his hands wouldn't stop shaking. The cold metal of the handcuffs bit into his wrists, a harsh reminder that this wasn't some bad dream or temporary setback.

This was real.

His mouth was dry. He tried swallowing, but his throat felt like sandpaper. The room was too small, too damn quiet—except for the faint muffled voices behind the two-way mirror. They'd been watching him for what felt like forever, letting him stew in his own sweat, waiting for him to break first.

But Kevin wasn't a rookie to pressure.

You been in tight spots before, bro. You'll get outta this.

Except this wasn't some street beef. This wasn't a client trying to stiff him on money.

This was feds, federal time, conspiracy charges—the kind of shit that didn't just go away.

He stared at the fingerprint-smudged metal table, mind racing.

How the fuck did I let it get this far?

He had seen the signs—the whispers in Philly, the subtle shifts in Isabella's tone, the uncle's lingering stares. And yet, he ignored them all. He thought he was smarter, slicker, thought he had control.

But the truth was, Kevin had been playing checkers in a game of chess, and now the board had collapsed beneath him.

A knot twisted in his stomach at the thought. He shook his head.

Hearing his mother Toni's voice and his brother Thomas's voice in his mind:

"You're going to get caught."

"Everything you worked hard for will go down the drain."

He thought about his daughter, Laylaa—about her crying face visiting him behind a glass window.

The disappointment.

The damage.

His leg bounced under the table. He needed answers.

Then, it happened.

A sound.

The door clicked open behind him—soft, deliberate.

He stiffened, fingers curling into fists.

The faint scent of perfume hit him first. Then, heels tapping lightly against the tile floor, slow and intentional, stopping just behind him.

He barely breathed.

Then, a voice—smooth, controlled, familiar.

"You were very lucky this time, Kevin."

His heart stopped.

That voice.

His chest tightened as his mind scrambled to place it, but it was impossible.

It couldn't be.

Slowly, his body tensed. His pulse roared in his ears.

And then it clicked.

Flashing back

The morning light in Miami spilled through the blinds as

Kevin rolled out of bed, rubbing the
sleep from his eyes. He checked his phone—three missed FaceTime calls from Laylaa. "Damn,"
he muttered, quickly dialing her back.
She picked up with a little attitude, "Nice of you to call back, Daddy."
"My bad, baby girl," he said, smiling. "I was up late with clients."
"You missed practice," she said, not hiding her disappointment.

"I know, I know. I owe you. But I'll be at your game this weekend—front row, flowers,
everything."
"Mmhm," she said with a half-smirk. "You better be."
They laughed, exchanged their secret code.
"Who are you?" he asked.
"Daddy's favorite person in the whole wide world," she answered, and Kevin's heart swelled.
After the call, he flipped open his appointment book. Fully stacked. But one name stood
out—Isabella. Just seeing her name made him grin. Wealthy, sexy, sharp, and always tipping

him like she was funding a scholarship.

As He dropped off a woman from the club that morning—just one of the many he used to entertain—but it didn't hit the same anymore. Their back-and-forth in the car was playful.

"By the way," she said, fixing her lip gloss, "my homegirl said you cute."

Kevin chuckled. "Tell her she can join you this weekend at the condo. Pool's open. Or maybe we'll do something'…private."

She gave him a sly look. "You wild."

"Only on Thursdays," he said with a wink, letting her out.

But his mind was on Isabella.

At the salon

The scent of product, burnt hair, and ambition filled the air as Kevin strolled into the salon.

Fresh lineup. New kicks. Confidence on a hundred.

Clients already filled the seats, chatter bouncing between stations. Kevin threw nods and daps
as he made his way to his chair.

he was already in rhythm doing clients when Isabella

walked in

She was impossible to miss.

Full-figured in all the right ways, her caramel skin glowing against the light flowy sundress she wore.

Her long, toned legs led to soft curves, and her thick, silky black hair framed a face that could stop traffic.

Everything about her screamed money and power, but she still carried herself like she wasn't trying too hard.

Kevin's mind flashed back to when she first told him she was from Bogotá, Colombia.

That accent. That flavor. It made her even harder to resist.

She flashed a soft smile as she sat in his chair. "I need the full Kevin experience today."

Kevin grinned. "You already know what it is."

He worked the shampoo bowl with skilled fingers, gently massaging her scalp.

Isabella closed her eyes, humming lightly. "Mmm. You should seriously think about offering full-body massages."

Kevin leaned down, murmuring close to her ear.

"I do. But those are private sessions."

She opened her eyes, catching his in the mirror. The look they shared was electric.

After the Service – The Invitation

Isabella admired her hair, running her fingers through it.

"You did your thing, as always."

She pulled a thick wad of bills from her designer purse and handed it to him, slipping an extra

hundred on top without blinking.

As Kevin swept the cash into his pocket, Isabella tilted her head.

"So… what's up with that private massage?"

Are you free this weekend?

He paused for a beat. Thinking about the potential threesome he had lined up for this weekend

& said " No im free" thinking to himself hes had many of threesomes in his day but there was

something special about Isabella!

She leaned in slightly, whispering, "Good. I'll text you."

They shared another loaded look, the kind that said this

wasn't just business anymore.

And just like that, Isabella turned and walked out of the salon, leaving Kevin standing there,

knowing damn well he wasn't ready for what was coming.

CHAPTER 2: THE YACHT DATE

Kevin finished the rest of his day with a noticeable lightness. Later that week, when the two girls from the nightclub hit him up to reschedule that potential threesome, he politely curved them.

That weekend, Isabella set the tone. Wear something nice," she texted. "My driver will pick you up in 30."

Kevin had no idea where he was going. The black SUV dropped him at a private dock.

Miami – Private Dock, Early Evening

The yacht was something out of a luxury lifestyle magazine—sleek, pristine, and massive. The kind of boat only a handful of people could afford to own. The gentle hum of the ocean surrounded it, the waves rocking gently against the dock as the golden sun began dipping below the horizon.

And there she was.

Isabella stood at the top of the entrance, leaning casually against the polished rail, the wind catching the hem of her silky sundress, making it flutter just enough to hint at the bikini underneath. Her toned legs stretched long and lean, her golden-brown skin glowing in the setting sun. Colombian perfection—Bogotá born and every bit as dangerous as she was beautiful.

She was barefoot, heels discarded nearby, her confidence making her even sexier.

"Come on up," she called with a slow smirk.

Kevin tightened the cuffs of his tailored linen shirt, adjusted his Rolex, and stepped onto the dock.

He wasn't new to nice things—but this?

This was different.

This was her world.

And tonight, he was stepping right into it.

The Yacht – Private Dinner & The First Hint

The inside of the yacht looked like something straight out of a billionaire's dream—marble counters, glass chandeliers, white leather seating sunken into the lounge. Soft Latin music floated in the air, mixing with the salty scent of the sea.

A private chef moved around the kitchen in crisp whites, carefully plating lobster tails and delicate sides. A waiter in black and white served drinks—top-shelf tequila, the kind that warmed without burning.

Kevin relaxed into one of the loungers, drink in hand, watching Isabella glide across the deck.

"You ever get tired of flying back and forth to Philly?" she asked casually, swirling her glass.

Kevin shrugged. "Nah. My daughter's there."

Isabella nodded, smiling just enough to show she remembered. "You told me before."

It wasn't a big moment. Just a detail tucked into the conversation. But it lingered—an invisible thread tying them closer.

The Night Turns Up – Passion on the Ocean

The tequila settled warm in Kevin's chest. The soft ocean breeze teased Isabella's hair, and the way she crossed her legs, slow and deliberate, nearly undid him.

She leaned in, brushing her fingers over his thigh as she whispered something low and sweet.

And that was all it took.

In a flash, his lips crashed against hers, hungry, claiming.

Her fingers dug into his shoulders as he lifted her, carrying her across the deck, finding the first

flat surface he could—a cushioned bench overlooking the ocean.

They didn't just have sex.

They wrecked each other.

Hands everywhere. Moans swallowed.

Her legs wrapped tightly around him.

His hand tangled in her hair.

Sweat slicked their skin, the ocean breeze cooling their bodies just enough before they collided

again, harder, deeper.

She wasn't delicate. She gave as good as she got.

And Kevin? He unleashed everything he'd been holding back.

When they collapsed side by side afterward, breathing hard, both staring up at the stars, Kevin

couldn't even remember the girls from the club anymore.

They weren't even close to this.

The Next Morning – The Pull Tightens

The yacht bobbed gently out at sea, the Miami skyline a thin line in the distance.

Kevin sat shirtless at the breakfast table, a spread of fresh fruit, eggs, smoked salmon, and
mimosas laid out in front of him.
Isabella sat across from him in a loose robe, her hair messy, her face glowing without a drop of
makeup.
He couldn't stop staring at her.
"You ever been to Philly before?" he asked, keeping his tone casual.
She smiled lazily. "I used to live there. With my uncle when I was younger."
Kevin arched a brow. "Yeah?"
"Yeah," she nodded, sipping her mimosa. "But I've been here for a while now. Miami's more my
speed."
She stretched her arms over her head, exposing just a glimpse of that bikini underneath. Kevin
had to fight to stay focused.
"Actually," she continued, "I've been thinking… I might have a little gift to send up to my uncle."

Kevin shrugged easily. "You want me to take it for you?"

Her smile was soft, almost sweet. "Would you? Just a little something. It's nothing crazy."

He nodded without thinking.

"No problem."

Just like that.

CHAPTER 3: THE FIRST DROP

The Next Few Days – The Shift Continues

After that weekend, Kevin moved different.

Not on purpose. Not because Isabella asked him to.

It just happened.

She'd text just enough to keep him thinking about her.

"Last night was unforgettable."

"You around this week?"

"I love your energy."

Meanwhile, the two girls from the club hit him up nonstop.

"So what happened? You stood us up!"

"We still down for that pool party?"

Kevin read the texts and locked his phone without answering.

No shade. No disrespect. He just wasn't interested anymore.

There was something about Isabella—the maturity, the danger, the way she made him feel

important and desired at the same time.

She wasn't like the others.

A Few Days Later – The Setup Moves Forward

They met again, this time at his condo.

No yacht. No fancy setups.

Just the two of them, raw and real.

Isabella showed up late—wearing tight jeans and a silky top that barely concealed her curves.

As soon as he opened the door, she was all over him.

Another night of pure fire.

Her body against his. Her nails down his back.

Kevin woke up the next morning thinking maybe, just maybe, he was in over his head—and

loving every second of it.

The Morning Before His Flight – The Package

Before heading to the airport, he swung by her condo one last time.

She greeted him at the door, wearing only a long t-shirt that barely covered her thighs.

Kevin barely made it inside before she dropped to her knees in front of him.

Her hands were confident. Her mouth was magic.

She took her time—working him slow, deep, deliberate—giving him head so good it made him see stars.

When he finally caught his breath, grinning like a fool, Isabella kissed his stomach, grabbed a

small package from her nightstand, and casually tucked it into his carry-on bag.

"Just drop it off for me," she whispered, zipping the bag closed.

Kevin didn't even hesitate.

"Yeah, I got you."

One last kiss, one last look.

Then he was out the door, thinking about her and nothing else.

No questions. No suspicions.

Just trust.

Miami Airport – Early Afternoon

Kevin stood off to the side of the TSA checkpoint, arms crossed and relaxed. He knew the drill

by now. Flying back and forth from Miami to Philly to do hair meant the scissors, razors, and

clippers in his carry-on always flagged the system.

"Sir, what's in the bag?" the TSA agent asked, barely looking up.

"Hair tools," Kevin said coolly. "I'm a stylist."

The agent opened the bag, glanced over the padded holsters and chrome instruments like it was his third time that day. "You always carry this?"

"Every trip," Kevin replied. "Gotta stay sharp."

"Fair enough."

But just as Kevin zipped the bag closed, a second agent—a woman this time—waved him over.

"We got a flag on your body scan," she said, lips twitching at the corners.

Kevin sighed. "Let me guess… no underwear again?"

She smiled. "You tell me."

He gave her a half-smirk. "Y'all gonna write me up or ask for my number?"

She laughed, cheeks slightly red. "You're clear, sir. But maybe next time, wear a layer."

He grabbed his bag and winked. "Maybe next time I don't fly solo."

Outside – Terminal Pickup Zone

The cold Philly air slapped him in the chest like a wet towel. Kevin winced, exhaling hard through his nose. "Jesus Christ," he muttered, tugging at his thin Miami hoodie like it could magically thicken up.

Even after all these back-and-forths, that first hit of Northeast air always got him. Miami had made him spoiled.

His breath fogged in front of him as he stepped toward the curb.

That's when he heard it.

"BRRRRRRRRMMM!!"

A black-on-black Charger pulled up hard, bass thumping so heavy it made the sidewalk vibrate.

Passenger window cracked. Smoke and heat escaped like the car had its own climate.

Telly leaned over the wheel, hoodie pulled low, gold frames tucked on his face like he never took 'em off.

"Damn, Kev, they cavity searched you again?" he called out, grinning.

Kevin slid into the passenger seat, shaking off the chill. "Nah, this time shorty just wanted to flirt.

No draws had her shook."

Telly laughed, dapped him up. "Some things never change."

They peeled off from the terminal, tires humming against the pavement.

Telly looked over. "So what's up? We shooting to Big Rube's first and grab cheesesteaks, or what?"

Kevin shook his head. "Nah, I gotta make a run first. Quick stop."

"Yeah? Where to?"

"Club Santuario."

Telly's face didn't move much, but Kevin caught it—the quick flicker of surprise. Like he recognized the name too well.

"That joint over off Passyunk?" Telly asked, casual.

"Yeah. Just gotta drop off a little gift for a friend."

Telly nodded slowly, eyes forward. "Bet. Santuario. Haven't been over there in a minute."

No follow-up questions. No jokes. Just that subtle shift in his face—one Kevin might've missed if he didn't know Telly as long as he had.

But he didn't press it.

Club Santuario – South Philly, Late Afternoon

The Charger slid up smooth to a quiet corner in South

Philly, where the air smelled like fried food and old secrets. Club Santuario didn't look like much from the outside—matte black walls, no sign, just a single gold "S" etched into a marble slab by the door.

But Kevin knew what he was looking at.

This wasn't no pop-up lounge. This was the kind of spot people whispered about. High ceilings, low lighting, and only a chosen few had the address saved in their phones.

"Damn," Kevin muttered, stepping out. "They doing it like this?"

Telly stayed behind the wheel, watching with that unreadable look again. "Welcome to the other side."

Kevin walked up slow, pulling his jacket tight. The club's front doors opened before he even knocked.

A large Spanish man in a black suit stepped forward, earpiece in his ear, eyes covered by dark shades despite the low light outside.

"Can I help you?" he asked, tone clipped.

"Yeah, I'm here to see Mr. Santiago," Kevin said, voice smooth but respectful. "I'm dropping off something for him. He knows."

The doorman didn't blink. "Mr. Santiago is busy at the moment. You can leave it with me."

Kevin hesitated for a half second—then slid the black leather pouch from under his coat and handed it over.

The man took it with both hands, nodding once. "It'll get where it needs to go."

Kevin turned to leave, no receipt, no confirmation—just trust.

As he slid back into the Charger, Telly didn't even ask. He just pulled off.

Big Rube's – North Philly, 30 Minutes Later

The smell hit first—onions grilled into submission, beef sizzling in long lines on the flat top.

Kevin's stomach growled the second they stepped inside.

"Now this," he said, grinning, "this is what I came home for."

Big Rube's was his go-to—always had been. Old-school counter service, greasy brown paper bags, and the kind of cheesesteaks that made grown men moan on the first bite.

Telly was already unwrapping his when they sat in the corner.

"Yo, you still dip yours in ketchup like a rookie?" he asked through a mouthful.

Kevin laughed. "Don't hate greatness."

They ate in silence for a few minutes, Philly playing softly in the background—Meek, Beans &
Freeway whatever the kitchen felt like today.

No mention of the gift.

No mention of Santuario.

Just steak, cheese, and the kind of silence only two old friends could share comfortably.

Next Day – Late Morning, West Philly

Kevin rolled through the city in a rented whip, windows down, portable hair kit riding shotgun.

He had time before Laylaa's recital that evening, so he booked 4 quick house call appointments.

Not just for the money, but to see some of his loyal day-ones—women who'd been booking him
since back when he had a cracked phone screen and was

still using public transit.

First stop: Carmen, a thick little thing with a slick tongue who always tipped in cash and compliments. She wanted her leave-out flat-ironed and her edges "laid like lace."

Kevin was mid-flat iron pass when his phone buzzed on the table. He glanced down.

Isabella:

Hey stranger. Just checking in. Everything go okay with the drop?

Kevin smirked and texted back with one hand while still working the section with the other.

Kevin:

Yeah my bad, meant to hit you last night. Got in, handled it clean.

Your uncle was busy so I passed it off to security.

My homie Telly dragged me out after that, had me running the Philly streets all night.

Just getting to my first client now. Got a full day…

Laylaa's recital later too.

Isabella:

Mmm. I like a man who can multitask.

Tell your daughter I said break a leg

Kevin grinned, tucking the phone away and turning back to Carmen.

"You good?" she asked, chewing gum and scrolling her phone.

"Always," he said, combing her leave-out smooth and clean. "Just gotta finish on time. I'm
already behind."

Afternoon – House Call Hustle

The second client ran late opening the door, the third one wanted "just a quick trim" that turned
into a whole damn silk press and edge repair.

By 4:30, Kevin was watching the clock like it owed him money. He still had to grab flowers and
haul ass across town.

"Alright, you good," he told the last client, handing her the mirror. "I gotta slide."

"Wait, you not gon' edge my baby hairs?"

Kevin kissed the air. "Next time, Queen. Daddy duty calls."

Evening – Sprint to the Recital

He hit the flower shop ten minutes before curtain call.

Grabbed the last decent bouquet—lavender and white, Laylaa's favorites—and peeled off toward the school like it was a race.

He parked crooked and jogged inside, bouquet in hand, hoodie half-zipped, breath tight in his chest.

He spotted Heather before she spotted him.

Hair pinned up, tight dress hugging all the right places. Her eyes said everything.

"You're always late," she whispered as he slid into the seat next to her.

Kevin leaned in and kissed her on the cheek. "Shut up, beautiful."

She rolled her eyes but he saw the corner of her mouth twitch.

The Recital

The lights dimmed.
Soft piano music played.
Laylaa stepped onto the stage in her glittery lavender outfit, hair curled, tiny tiara sparkling under the spotlight.

Kevin's heart swelled.

He didn't record it on his phone. He just watched.

Just felt it.

When the music ended, he clapped loud and proud, standing up before anyone else.

Laylaa ran to him after the show, glowing and breathless.

"Who are you?" he asked, kneeling down.

She grinned wide. "Daddy's favorite person in the whole wide world."

He handed her the flowers. "Always."

Dinner – Family Vibes & Business Buzz

They hit a little family-style spot after the recital—Laylaa's pick, of course. Fried chicken, mashed potatoes, macaroni & cheese that tasted like somebody's auntie made it.

Kevin cracked jokes, made Laylaa laugh, and slid a few soft compliments at Heather—nothing heavy.

"You still got that walk," he said between bites.

Heather gave him the side-eye. "You still got that mouth."

He smiled and sipped his drink.

Between bites, Kevin finally replied to Isabella's earlier message.

Kevin:

She did great. Flowers, glitter, whole production.

I'm out to dinner with them now.

Appreciate you checking in.

A few seconds later, the typing dots popped up.

Isabella:

I love that. You're a good dad, Kevin.

I'll make sure to reward you next time I see you 💋

Kevin smirked, tucked the phone away, and reached across the table to steal a bite of Laylaa's mac and cheese.

"Hey!" she giggled, swatting at his hand.

Heather shook her head, amused.

It was one of those moments — rare, unbothered, and full of simple joy.

No pressure.

No worries.

Just life vibing how it should

Chapter 4:

Double Life

Miami – a few Months Later

Kevin moved different now. Not because he was trying to — it just happened naturally.

His schedule was tight, money was flowing, and for once, things felt… balanced.

Clients hit him up daily. House calls, salon appointments, private styling sessions for photo shoots. He was booked solid from sunup to late night.

His hands stayed in heads, and his pockets stayed full.

And when he wasn't working?

He was with Isabella.

Two, sometimes three or four times a week, she'd pop up on him — silk dress, perfume floating in the air, some new earrings, another expensive pair of heels Red Bottoms, like it was nothing.

Sometimes they'd chill in his condo. Other times, she'd send a driver and have him meet her at some rooftop spot he never heard of before that night. Sushi bars with private booths. Latin lounges with live bands and cocktails that cost more than some people's phone bills.

She always smelled like she belonged to a higher tax bracket.

But what had Kevin really leaning in… was the way she made him feel like he belonged there

too.

Ignored Calls, Missed Opportunities

Women he used to mess with — women who used to be his "whenever" crew — started texting

again. Maybe it was the way he was posting now. The way his name was moving around.

Tasha:

"You still in Miami or nah? I need my ends trimmed 🙄"

Jasmine:

"We still doing that pool day or you forgot about me?"

Alina:

"Don't act brand new, Kev."

He'd glance at the messages, smile, then lock his phone without replying.

He wasn't in that mode anymore.

They didn't hold his attention.

Isabella did.

One Morning – His Condo

Kevin stood in the kitchen shirtless, brushing waves into his hair with one hand, sipping coffee with the other. His phone lit up on the counter.

Isabella:

"You're becoming a bad habit. I keep wanting to see you."

He smirked and texted back.

Kevin:

"Who said I want you to quit?"

She replied with a picture — just her legs, crossed, with a wine glass in hand.

Isabella:

"Can I pull up later?"

Kevin:

"Door unlocked."

Clientele Climbing

He used the extra money to reinvest:

- Bought a new cordless clipper set
- Upgraded his salon chair to one with chrome legs and memory foam
- Got his name stitched into his barber smock in gold

thread

He even bought himself a new pair of Balenciagas and a bottle of Creed — "just because".

And nobody questioned it.

Because Kevin still worked.

He didn't quit hair.

He just started living better.

Toni's Call – Something in Her Spirit

It was a Tuesday morning when the phone rang. His mother's name flashed across the screen:

Toni Gaskins.

"Hey Ma," he answered, still halfway asleep.

There was a pause before she spoke.

"You good, baby?"

"Yeah, I'm good. Just tired. Long week."

"You sure?" she said slower this time. "I don't know… something in my spirit been feelin' off lately."

Kevin sat up.

"Off how?"

"I had a dream," she said. "Not one of those goofy ones. One of the ones that stick. Just want you to be careful."

Kevin smiled to himself.

"Aight, Ma. I got you. I'm good though, I promise."

"You better be," she replied. "And stop ignoring my texts, boy. I ain't one of your little girlfriends."

He laughed. "Yes ma'am."

Chapter 4: Double Life (Part 2)

—

Wednesday Night – Kevin's Condo

Kevin had just finished cleaning his clippers when he heard the knock at the door.

It wasn't loud — more like a soft tap, like she didn't want to disturb the peace that already lived inside.

He opened the door.

Isabella stood there in jeans, sneakers, and a fitted hoodie — no heels, no makeup, no designer bag. Just her.

Kevin tilted his head, surprised. "You alright?"

She nodded and walked in slowly, like her spirit was heavy but she didn't want to say it out loud yet. Kevin closed the door behind her.

They sat on the couch for a few minutes in silence. Then she finally said it.

"It's my mom's birthday this week."

Kevin leaned back. "Damn. I didn't know. You never talk about her."

She looked at him with this far-off expression. "Her and my dad… both of their birthdays are in May. Same month. Couple weeks apart."

She picked at the cuff of her sleeve. "They died when I was a little girl."

Kevin sat up straighter.

"Car accident," she continued. "We were all in the car… I don't remember most of it. Just that we flipped. A few times. I woke up in the hospital asking for them… and nobody wanted to tell me the truth."

Kevin leaned in closer, listening.

"They were both gone," she said quietly. "My mom's brother — my uncle — flew down to get me and brought me back to Philly. That's who raised me. That's why we're close."

Kevin placed his hand on her leg, gentle. "I'm sorry. For real."

She gave him a soft smile, like she appreciated the words but had already heard them from too

many people who didn't really care. This time was different, though.

Kevin did care.

After a pause, she reached into her bag and pulled out a small, black shoe box sized gift

"I have something for my uncle ," she said. "A gift. Just something little… sentimental. You said

you're heading to Philly this weekend, right?"

Kevin nodded. "Yeah, I got a couple clients to hit. Layla has her soccer game too."

"If you don't mind… can you drop this off to him? Same spot."

Kevin took it without hesitation. The gifts had become a monthly thing as he traveled to Philly.

"Of course," he said. "Ain't nothin'."

She leaned her head against his shoulder.

"I just like doing nice things for him… especially this time of year."

Kevin didn't say much after that. Just held her, rubbed her back with his fingers while she closed her eyes and melted into the silence.

He wasn't thinking about any red flags.

He wasn't calculating anything.

He was just in it.

And to him…

it felt good to be needed.

Chapter 5: THE WARNING

The TSA girl was waiting. Same curly ponytail, same sly smile, same latex gloves. Kevin
stepped into the scanner, arms raised, trying to keep a straight face.
"You're back again , once a month huh?" she teased, eyes scanning him as much as the
machine did.
He smirked. "Work never stops."
"I see," she said, slowly stepping forward. "You know I gotta pat you down again. Arms out."

Kevin didn't flinch. This time, she let her fingers linger just a little longer near his
waistband—before tapping him lightly right on the balls.
"Ma'am," he said playfully, "you tryna get me caught up out here?"
She whispered, "That's your warning shot," and winked, waving him through.
Same game, every time.
Another smooth flight!
Out front, the Philly air was finally warmer. No more layering up like February. May brought that

first sweat when you moved too fast in a hoodie.

As Kevin rolled his suitcase across the pickup lane, a sleek black sedan pulled up. The window rolled down — it was Don in the passenger seat, flashing a grin.

"What's up, city boy?" Don called out.

Kevin smirked. "Y'all missed me that bad, huh?"

Telly leaned over from the driver's seat. "Man, hop in. We got things to do."

Kevin tossed his bag in the trunk and slid into the back. The seats were soft, cool leather. He noticed it was a different car this time—still nice, but not the old ride Telly usually drove.

"New wheels?" Kevin asked.

"Something light," Telly shrugged. "Where we heading? Cheesesteaks first, pool hall, or you got another one of those mysterious stops to make?"

Kevin chuckled. "Actually, yeah. I gotta swing by that spot again—drop off a little something for Isabella's uncle."

Telly's brow twitched, just slightly. Don glanced at Telly, then back at Kevin in the rearview.

"You really locked in with shorty, huh?" Don said. Kevin nodded, eyes lighting up. "Man, she bad. I'm talkin' flawless skin, that Colombian accent… Money long, nails done, hair always on point thanks to me of course! She even been blessing me with gifts. Real ones. Shit, she bought me a watch last week I don't even wanna wear in public."

Telly kept driving, but Kevin could feel the temperature shift in the car. That unsaid tension. Telly was quiet, thinking two or three steps ahead—because that's what street dudes do. And Kevin? Kevin was just floating in the clouds of lust and new attention.

"Whereyou want me to pull up out front or out back? Telly finally asked.

"Out back" Kevin replied "its early the front door still locked"

Telly gave a low whistle. "You really like her, huh."

Kevin shrugged. "She different, bro."

Don leaned back. "You ever wonder what's in them boxes?"

Kevin laughed. "Nah, it's her uncle. She said she just likes to send him gifts since he raised her after her parents passed."

Telly gave Don a look. Don responded with a quiet: "Mmm."

No one said much else. But the vibe in the car was undeniable.

They pulled up to the club again. Kevin went in alone. The security at the back door recognized him immediately and gave him a nod.

"Wait here," one of them said, before disappearing into the velvet-draped corridor. Moments later, he returned. "He'll see you now."

Kevin followed him inside. The back hallway was lined with imported stone, candles glowing in sleek wall sconces. It smelled like money. Power. Oddly Danger.

Inside a private lounge sat Isabella's uncle—a sharp-suited man with salt-and-pepper hair, perfectly trimmed beard, and a scar slicing down near his jawline. He didn't get up, but his presence filled the room.

"Kevin," the man said, extending his hand.

Kevin shook it. Firm grip. Eyes locked.

"So… you're the one my niece is always talking about."

Kevin offered a respectful smile. "Yes, sir. She's a special woman."

"She is," the uncle nodded. "Like a daughter to me. I raised her when her parents passed. I'm

very… protective." Giving Kevin a hard serious stare.

Kevin nodded, staying composed.

"She told me yall have been spending a lot of time together," the uncle said, glancing over at his security. It's good to see she has someone dependable. But let me give you some advice,

man-to-man. Don't play games with my niece ."

Kevin nodded again. "I don't."

The uncle leaned forward, voice low. "Make sure you don't."

It wasn't a threat. But it wasn't a casual warning either.

Security stood by the door, arms folded.

The air felt thick. Kevin felt the weight of it all.

He handed over the gift box and stepped out, breathing a little deeper once he hit the Philly night air.

Back in the car, Don looked over. "So... how was the meet-the-family moment?"

Kevin exhaled. "Man... I see where she gets it from." They all laughed.

"Alright," Telly said. "Let's hit Mosconi to shoot pool."

The pool hall smelled like cigar smoke, chalk dust, and Italian pride. Kevin chalked his cue
lazily while Telly racked up the balls like it was second nature. Don leaned over a high-top table
sipping from a plastic cup of ginger ale, watching them shoot with a smirk.

"So this Isabella girl," Don started casually, "She the reason you lookin' like a million bucks
now?"

Kevin grinned, lining up his shot. "Man, don't hate. Appreciate. You should see her in person.
Fine don't even cut it. She got that real money, but humble with it. Smart. Sexy. She keep me on
my toes." Sexy ass Columbian

Don raised an eyebrow. "Mmm. So what's up with the gift you dropped off earlier? You ain't even know what was in it?"

Telly didn't look up from his shot, but his silence spoke volumes.

Kevin shrugged. "Man, it was a favor. Her uncle raised her. She said it was just something nice she wanted to do for him. Birthday gift or something. What's the big deal?"

Telly finally sank a ball, then straightened up and gave Kevin a long look. "No big deal. Just… you makin' runs for people you don't know, in places you ain't familiar with. All I'm sayin' is—be smart. Sometimes things look sweet till they rot from the inside out."

Kevin laughed it off. "Y'all tryna kill my vibe. I'm cool. I ain't stupid."

Don leaned in, tapping the edge of the table with his ring. "We ain't sayin' you stupid. We sayin' you in love. And love got a funny way of making smart dudes blind as hell."

The next morning , Kevin parked his rental near the community soccer field. Spring had finally warmed up Philly, and the grass was vibrant green under the golden sun. He walked up just in

time to catch Laylaa on the field—her ponytail bouncing as she hustled past a defender. Kevin
smiled wide.

He found a seat near the front, placing the bouquet of pink and blue flowers on the bench next

to him. Heather was already there, arms crossed, giving him that classic Heather look—the one

that said, you late again, fool. She was in a sundress and hoops, pretty but unimpressed.

Kevin leaned over and kissed her cheek. "Shut up, beautiful," he whispered with a grin. She
rolled her eyes but didn't move away.

The game played on, but Kevin noticed someone across the field—someone watching him. A

tall dude in designer sneaks, fitted jeans, and a muscle tee, holding a little kid's hand. The guy

whispered to his girl and shot Kevin a look.

Kevin clocked it instantly—an ex's new man. He thought to himself oh she messing with Dre

now. One of them ones who always knew too much and

nothing at all. Probably knee more then he needed to know about Kevin through pillow talk. Probably thinking we got beef now that he messing with 1 of my ex's. His jaw clenched as he turned his focus back to the game.

Laylaa scored a goal near the end, and Kevin jumped up clapping. She looked toward the sideline, grinning, and he shouted, "Who are you?!"

Laylaa beamed. "Daddy's favorite person in the whole wide world!"

He jogged to the field's edge with the flowers. "You killed it, mama," he said, pulling her into a hug. Heather actually smiled at that.

They all grabbed a bite to eat afterward—nothing fancy, just laughs and love. But the look from that dude Dre at the field lingered in the back of Kevin's mind, like a whisper in a crowded room.

Chapter 6: The Weight of the Bag

Back in Miami, everything still felt like a dream. Kevin and Isabella were deep in their groove—dinners on the water, spontaneous club nights, slow mornings wrapped in sheets, and skin. Their chemistry was magnetic. Her world wrapped around his like silk, luxurious and light, yet the thread was starting to tighten in ways he didn't quite notice—yet.

A few days after their last Philly trip, Isabella surprised him again.

"I got you something," she said, walking into the living room wearing nothing but an oversized t-shirt and wet hair from the shower. She dropped a black leather duffel bag onto the couch in front of him. Sleek, heavy-duty. The kind of bag that made you feel official. Vélez Leather bag

"For your hair tools," she said. "I figured you could step your travel game up."

Kevin unzipped it and whistled. "Damn. This joint look like it belong to a whole assassin."

She smiled. "Well, you do kill it , don't you?"
It was bigger than his usual travel bag. Slick black leather, reinforced sides, high-end zippers. It felt like money. A High end Columbian brand.
"When you go to Philly this time, i only have a letter for my uncle. If you dont mind taking it to him please?

Sure no gifts this time? he asked casually.
She waved him off. "No, no gift. I just want you to go see him, spend a little time with him. I think he likes you. That's rare." Plus he loves that Velez brand make sure you show it to him…
Kevin nodded slowly, tucking that 1 thought away … that me showing a man a bag that had money was a little weird.
At the airport, it was the same old story.
The flirty TSA agent spotted him in line and lit up.
"Well, well. If it isn't Mr. Magic Hands."
He smirked. "You really need to pat me down again?"
"Regulations," she said, with a wink, before deliberately running her hands a little too slow and

tapping him lightly between the legs.

"Mmhmm. Still not wearing underwear."

Kevin laughed. "You gotta stop fallin' in love at work, ma."

When he landed in Philly, the air was hot now. August had sun had the heat on hell.

He stepped out of the terminal just in time to see a slick charcoal Audi pull up.

Chapter 7
All the Signs

It was Telly and Don picked him up from the airport, this time in a different ride—sleek, black, still flossy, Audi.

"Damn, y'all switch whips more than I switch chicks," Kevin joked as he slid into the back seat.

Telly smirked. "Gotta keep the look fresh."

Kevin was glowing. "Yo, I'm tellin' you—this girl Isabella… she the truth. She got it all—class, sex appeal, and she be treatin' a brother right. Bought me this bag, gave me bread, and bro… she don't stop."

Telly glanced at Don, who stayed quiet. Kevin didn't notice the look they shared in the rearview mirror.

"You still droppin' off that gift?" Don asked casually.

"Yeah. Said her uncle likes me . She gave me an envelope to drop off," Kevin replied.

Don chuckled under his breath. "Damn, you doin' deliveries now?"

Telly laughed, but the tone was off. "What's in the envelope?"

"Man, I ain't check. You know how that go," Kevin shrugged.

Telly looked at him hard. "I don't. Nigga"

Kevin brushed it off. "She Columbian you know they do family different from us.

They pulled up to the club—Don said "how come we never hit this Jawn when we were coming

up?" " Telly said shit i did every other weekend when yall nut asses was in the house boo loving.

With yall girls..".

Kevin stepped in and handed his bag over to security without a word — routine by now. While

they checked it, he hit the bathroom like usual.

When he came back out, the guard passed the bag back.

Kevin grabbed it, but something felt

off.

Light. Lighter than before.

He didn't react. Just threw it over his shoulder and kept it moving.

In the next room, the uncle was already waiting.

Kevin dapped him up and pulled the envelope from his jacket.

"From her," he said simply.

The uncle took it with a nod.

Then his tone shifted. "You know, a woman like her… been through a lot. She needs stability.

Loyalty. A man who knows what he's doing."

Kevin kept his face cool, but the tension was thick.

"I appreciate that. I take good care of her."

"I hope so," the uncle said. "This world is dangerous when people play games."

Security stood behind him, silent but watching. Kevin felt it in his throat—a hard swallow. This

was a message. He didnt even care about seeing the bag. Kevin got back in the car with Don and Telly, who were waiting nearby.

"How it go?" Don asked.

Kevin exhaled. "He's intense. Real mob vibes."

They drove Ball Buster a pool hall in south west As they shot a few racks, Don cracked the

silence.

"So let me get this straight—you carryin' bags, deliverin' envelopes, takin' trips… and you don't

know nothin'?"

Kevin chalked his cue. "What you tryna say?"

"I'm sayin'," Don continued, "you sure you not gettin' played, bro?"

Telly added, "You ever check that bag? I mean, you say it's for hair tools… but did you actually check it?"

Kevin shrugged. "Man, y'all buggin'. She solid."

They let it go—for now—but the air was heavy.

The next day, Kevin showed up to Laylaa's soccer game, bouquet in hand. She ran up, hugged him tight, beaming.

"Daddy!"

"Who are you?" he asked.

"Daddy's favorite person in the whole wide world!" she grinned.

They watched the next game together. But Kevin noticed Dre again & some dude named Mark with him

They didn't say anything, but their face said it all: suspicion, envy, calculated.

After the game, Kevin took Laylaa to dinner, joked with

his ex, and tried to ignore the weird energy—but it lingered.

Kevin boarded the plane with a lot on his mind.
Something was changing.
Something he couldn't quite name.
But it was already in motion.

Chapter 7 The Switch

Kevin touched back down in Miami like he never left.
The palm trees were swaying, the heat was thicker, and Isabella was waiting for him, posted up by her sleek black car in a silk wrap dress and shades that screamed luxury.
She kissed him soft and slow, then pulled a brand-new pair of sneakers out her trunk . "I got this for you. Figured you would like them .
"Damn," Kevin said. "You spoil me."
"You deserve it," she replied with a smile that didn't quite hit her eyes.
Are you hungry Isabella asked there's a Columbian restaurant not to far from here.
The place is vibrant but classy — wood tables, rich aromas, soft Latin music in the background.

ISABELLA

You like them?

KEVIN (grinning)

They fire. You didn't have to do all that.

Kevin steps away from the table, heading toward the restrooms. As he turns the corner,

someone else is walking out.

They almost bump into each other.

TIFFANY.

Time freezes for a half second.

She looks up, surprised — then a slow smile spreads.

TIFFANY

Well damn.

Kevin grins, speechless at first.

KEVIN

Tiff.

They don't say much — just fall into a long, soft hug.

Not rushed. Not casual. A hug with history.

When they pull back, she lightly touches his arm.

TIFFANY

You still smell the same.

Kevin chuckles. She glances past him, spotting Isabella at the table.

TIFFANY (smiling)

She's beautiful. I see your taste hasn't changed.

KEVIN

Neither has yours.

A soft beat. Neither one wants to leave just yet.

TIFFANY

It's good to see you, Kev.

KEVIN

Same here, Tiff.

They step apart slowly — a goodbye with weight, eyes saying more than their mouths do. Kevin watches her walk away for just a second too long… then exhales, adjusts his chain, and heads to the bathroom

Later that night, as they were laying in bed, she reached over to her nightstand and handed him an envelope.

I know your going right back to Philly next week for your Solid Gold Hair Shoot

"Can you give this to my uncle next time you go?"

Kevin, eyes half-shut, nodded. "Yeah, yeah… when?"

Then she said. It again Spend some time with him too. He really likes you. Said you got good energy."

He smirked. "He ain't say that with his face."

She giggled, but again—it felt hollow.

Kevin pretended to fall asleep that night. When she got up and slipped into the closet with his new bag, he peeked through squinted lids. She was smooth, She opened a false bottom in the bag—a hidden compartment layered so clean it looked seamless.

She slid in the bricks. Cocaine. Carefully stacked. Then closed it up like nothing ever happened.

Kevin didn't say a word. But thinking what Don & Telly were right all along. Pissed off thinking about his freedom & all he could lose & at the same time thinking oh the trying to play me well i got something for them…

The next day when He got home and dropped the bag on the couch. Sat down. Looked at it for a second, then leaned forward and unzipped it slow. Started pulling out the weight.

One by one, he tapped each brick of cocaine—wrapping them tight, sealed, clean. Thinking

payment for playing with me!

He stacked them back in the bag then closed the bag like nothing ever happened.

Hes week went pass easily like a typically did. TSA didnt even stop him this Flight . Telly and

Don weren't available to scoop him from the airport in Philly. So Kevin Ubered straight to the

uncle's spot solo.

Same protocol. Security waiting at the gate. This time, the guard stepped forward and took his

bag—aggressively first time that ever happened.

"You can give it back when I'm done," Kevin said, playing it cool.

Inside, the uncle greeted him like last time, still cold but more direct.

"You brought me something?"

Kevin handed him the envelope.

"Appreciate it," the uncle said flatly. "How's my niece?"

"She's good."

"You two still close?"

Kevin nodded. "Yeah."

"Then be careful," the uncle said. "You know what she's been through."

"I do."

They sat for a bit, talked lightly—sports, music, Colombia, Philly. When it was time to go, the guard returned his bag.

Kevin felt it instantly.

It was lighter.

He kept his face steady. Nodded a thank you. Walked out.

As soon as he got back to the Airbnb, he unzipped the bottom.

Empty.

She'd loaded it. Security had unloaded it.

He called Don later that night. "Yo, I got somethin' you might be interested in…"

By the next morning, Don was already on the move. Kevin cut the product and flipped it to Don at a crazy low price—quietly moving weight without

Isabella or her uncle knowing. Don put his young boys on it—Mark, JB, and Dre—who pushed it through their smaller Philly lanes.

A few more runs followed. Kevin played it slick—acting clueless, smiling on cue, handing off envelopes while letting them slip the weight into his bag like he didn't know.

But now he checked every time.

This wasn't a love story anymore. This was a hustle.

A silent one.

But not one without risk.

Because TSA had been watching.

And so had Don and them.

Everybody was watching now.

And everybody had questions.

Kevin just kept smiling.

Because now?

He had answers.

Chapter 8
Warnings in the Wind

Back in Miami, Kevin was living it up—but his mind was racing.

Isabella was still playing her role. Still sexy. Still sweet. Still seductive. But Kevin now saw the

cracks in the act. The bags. The bricks. The way her eyes didn't linger like they used to. Her

touches were softer… and less frequent.

She handed him another envelope one morning, barely dressed, sipping her tea like it was

nothing.

"This time, there's no gift. I just want you to go see my uncle. Spend some time with him. Keep

the relationship strong."

Kevin nodded, eyes on her, watching her more than he ever had. She wasn't the same girl he

first washed hair for in his chair. This Isabella had layers. & Secrets.

And he wasn't sure if he was sleeping with a lover… or a trap.

Kevin didn't even blink. He knew what that bag was now. Knew she'd pack it while he was in the shower. Knew she'd tuck it all in beneath the false bottom like it was part of her morning routine.

He didn't stop her.

Instead, he got smarter.

Before every flight, Kevin now carefully checked the bag after she packed it. Every time he

found drugs, he'd re-wrap them tight, reseal the hidden flap, and act like he didn't know. Then

he'd call Don.

"Yo. I got another one."

Don would slide through with his new whip and scoop it up like it was nothing. Mark, JB, and

Dre were in full distribution mode now. Don didn't ask too many questions… yet.

But he was watching.

Kevin started noticing the changes.

Don's pauses before he spoke.

Mark's sidelong glances.

JB and Dre sticking around longer than necessary, like they were studying him.

Kevin didn't say much. Just peeped the shift. Kept his guard up. But the red flags were everywhere now.

Even TSA was acting strange. At the Miami airport, the same flirty TSA agent who always let him slide was now getting hands-on.

"Let me pat you down personally," she said with a grin.

She tapped him on his inner thigh—then not-so-subtly tapped his balls.

Kevin smirked, played it off. "You got a thing for stylists, huh?"

But he clocked it.

She wasn't just being freaky anymore.

She was being thorough.

Back in Philly, he was solo again. This time, he pulled up to the uncle's compound in an Uber.

When he arrived, same routine: security greeted him, took the bag, and led him in. Kevin handed the envelope to Isabella's uncle, calm as ever.

But the tension in the room was different.

This time, the uncle's posture shifted. His tone changed.

You good?" the uncle asked.

Always," Kevin replied coolly.

You ever lie to my niece?"

No."

Ever lie to me?"

Kevin looked him in the eye. "Never had a reason to."

The uncle stared for a long moment… then nodded toward a nearby door.

Two of his security guards dragged out one of their own—bloodied, bruised, and limp I don't like thieves," the uncle said.

Before Kevin could react, they started beating the man in front of him. No questions. No mercy.

Kevin stood still, heart pounding, but face neutral. He didn't flinch.

Because he knew exactly what this was.

A message.

He left the club that day with a lighter bag and a heavier conscience.

Don and Telly were on high alert.

They didn't say anything to Kevin directly, but the air was thick with suspicion.

Telly kept it light, cracking jokes, but his eyes said everything. Don was colder now, quieter.

Watching every move Kevin made.

Nobody said it out loud.

But everybody was thinking the same thing:

Is Kevin setting us up?

Or is he being set up?

Either way… the storm was coming.

And Kevin could feel the wind shifting.

Chapter 9

The Storm Tightens

Kevin's days in Miami were still filled with sunlight, sex, and scissors. Isabella was still around,
still beautiful, still affectionate—but something had changed.
She started being short on calls. She didn't laugh as much. Her eyes would drift off in thought
mid-conversation. When Kevin asked if she was good, she'd nod with a soft, "Yeah, just tired."
He knew better.
The energy was different. And not just with her.
Back in Philly, Don, Mark, JB, and Dre were moving more product than ever—courtesy of
Kevin's drops. The packages kept coming, and the price Don paid was low enough that
everyone was eating good. But trust was thinning out.
Don wasn't stupid.
Every time Kevin delivered a package, Don was watching his movements closer.
Every time they broke down a brick, he looked for inconsistencies.
The problem? There were none.

Kevin was too smart. Too seasoned. Too careful.

He skimmed just enough. Not too much to get noticed, just enough to pocket a few thousand each time and keep the supply chain moving. So he thought

But nobody trusted a perfect game for too long.

And that's when TSA made their move.

After another Miami-to-Philly flight, Kevin was pulled aside again at the airport.

Same flirty TSA agent.

Same smile.

But this time, her badge was already in her hand.

"Step over here for me."

The pat-down was different—more thorough, more mechanical.

Kevin kept it cool. Played dumb. Said all the right things.

They didn't find anything that day, but the look in their eyes told him the surveillance was real now. The game had officially turned federal.

And it wasn't just TSA.

Chapter 10 -The Sting.

Kevin arrived in Philly like normal. Same routine. Same bag. Same envelope. Only this time, the
FBI had already been tipped off. TSA had flagged the bag during Kevin's last trip—he just didn't
know it yet.
As he approached the uncle's club unmarked vans surrounded the block. Tactical agents in
black poured out like shadows.
Don, Dre, JB, and Mark watched it all go down from a distance—engine running, eyes wide.
"Yo," JB muttered. "They locking that nigga up."
"Shit," Mark whispered. "We was just about to hit that spot."
Don exhaled. "Glad we didn't. That would've been our ass too."
From the back of the van, Dre said it again—quieter this time.
"Colombian motherfuckers too…"

Interrogation room
Kevin sat there, wrists cuffed, sweat beading at his forehead.

Everything was a blur. Stomach twisted thinking about him mom & Laylaa

Until he heard a familiar voice.

"You're lucky this time." Kev

He looked up.

It was Tiffany.

His ex.

His first real love.

Now a full-fledged federal agent.

She looked tired. He looked ashamed.

"You still doing hair?" she asked, folding her arms.

Kevin nodded.

"Good. You got talent. You always did. Don't waste it again."

Then she leaned in, whispered something no mic could pick up.

And hugged him.

Longer than protocol allowed.

"You're done," she said. "Now go live like it."

Final Scene – The Thankful File

Kevin rushed straight to Laylaa's house

He didn't know what deal Tiffany pulled, or how deep

she had to go. But everyone else got locked up—Isabella, her uncle, Somehow, Kevin walked away untouched.

But the guilt? That stuck around.

All he could think about was Layla. Her soccer games. Her shy little voice asking, "Who are you?"

"Daddy's favorite person in the whole wide world," he'd whisper back.

He thought about his mom, Toni. About the dream she had—the gut feeling something was off.

About his brother Thomas, who always warned him: Don't get pulled back into the street. You might not come out this time.

He thought about Don and Telly. How they peeped it before he did.

And he thought about the mirror.

What he saw.

And what almost got lost in the reflection.

Kevin took a long breath, and drove off with nothing in the trunk but his tools.

Hair tools.

No coke.

No packages.

No lies.

Just life.

The End.

Made in the USA
Middletown, DE
12 November 2025